Dear Parent:
Your child's love of reading starts here!

Every child learns to read in a different way and at his or her own speed. You can help your young reader improve and become more confident by encouraging his or her own interests and abilities. You can also guide your child's spiritual development by reading stories with biblical values and Bible stories, like I Can Read! books published by Zonderkidz. From books your child reads with you to the first books he or she reads alone, there are I Can Read! books for every stage of reading:

SHARED READING
Basic language, word repetition, and whimsical illustrations, ideal for sharing with your emergent reader.

BEGINNING READING
Short sentences, familiar words, and simple concepts for children eager to read on their own.

READING WITH HELP
Engaging stories, longer sentences, and language play for developing readers.

READING ALONE
Complex plots, challenging vocabulary, and high-interest topics for the independent reader.

ADVANCED READING
Short paragraphs, chapters, and exciting themes for the perfect bridge to chapter books.

I Can Read! books have introduced children to the joy of reading since 1957. Featuring award-winning authors and illustrators and a fabulous cast of beloved characters, I Can Read! books set the standard for beginning readers.

A lifetime of discovery begins with the magical words **"I Can Read!"**

Visit www.icanread.com for information on enriching your child's reading experience.
Visit www.zonderkidz.com for more Zonderkidz I Can Read! titles.

Anger is cruel, and wrath is like a flood,
but jealousy is even more dangerous.
—*Proverbs 27:4*

To Cassie Hendren
–*D.D.M.*

ZONDERKIDZ

A Perfect Pony
Copyright © 2011 by Dandi Daley Mackall
Illustrations copyright © 2011 by Claudia Wolf

Requests for information should be addressed to:
Zonderkidz, *Grand Rapids, Michigan* 49530

Library of Congress Cataloging-in-Publication Data

Mackall, Dandi Daley.
    A perfect pony / Dandi Daley Mackall ; illustrated by Claudia Wolf.
        p. cm. — (Horse named Bob)
    Summary: Jen and her best friend, Dave, have been having fun riding Bob the retired plow horse together, but when Dave gets a pretty pony for his birthday, Jen becomes jealous.
    ISBN 978-0-310-71783-6 (softcover)
    [1. Horses—Fiction. 2. Ponies—Fiction. 3. Friendship—Fiction. 4. Jealousy—Fiction. 5. Christian life—Fiction.] I. Wolf, Claudia, ill. II. Title.
PZ7.M1905Per 2011
    [E]—dc22   2009037511

Printed in China

11 12 13 14 15 /SCC/ 7 6 5 4 3 2 1

A Perfect Pony

story by Dandi Daley Mackall

pictures by Claudia Wolf

Jen's best friend was Bob the Horse.

Bob was Mrs. Gray's horse.

Jen took care of him.

She brushed Bob.

And she loved Bob the Horse.

"You are the best!" she told Bob.

Jen's other best friend was Dave.

Dave loved horses, too.

On the bus after school Jen asked,

"Do you want to ride Bob today?"

Dave answered, "Yes!"

"Bob is the best," Dave said.

"I love to ride Bob!"

Jen and Dave rode Bob the Horse.
Mrs. Gray showed them how to
get on big Bob from the fence.

Sometimes Jen rode in front.

Sometimes Dave rode in front.

"Faster!" Dave shouted.

But big Bob did not go fast.

The next day was Dave's birthday.

Dave opened Jen's gift first.

"A picture of Bob! Thanks, Jen,"

Dave said.

10

They ate cake and ice cream.

Then Dave's dad said,

"You have one gift left, Dave."

"Surprise!" said Dave's dad and mom.

"A pony!" Dave shouted.

"Wow!" Jen said. "She is so pretty!"

"Her name is Lily," said Dave's mom.

"You are the prettiest horse

I've ever seen!" Dave said.

All the kids agreed, even Jen.

Jen walked home to feed Bob.

Her mother helped carry hay.

"Dave got a pony for his birthday,"

Jen said. "Lily is so pretty."

"I am happy for Dave," Mom said.

Jen was happy for Dave.

But she wished she had a pony, too.

At lunch Jen asked Dave,

"Do you want to ride Bob today?"

"Why would he ride Bob?"

Erin asked. "He has his own pony.

Don't you wish you had a pony

like pretty Lily?"

"Where's your friend Dave?"

Mrs. Gray asked later that day.

"He is not coming," Jen said.

Jen tried to make Bob run,

but Bob only walked.

"Look!" Mrs. Gray said.

"Here comes Dave now.

That new pony can really run fast."

18

"Lily runs very fast," Jen said.

"Lily is so pretty.

Everybody thinks Lily is perfect.

I'll bet Dave is here to make fun

of you and me," Jen told Bob.

"Hi, Jen! How's Bob?" Dave asked.

"Just fine," Jen said.

"He sure looks big," Dave said.

That did it. "Oh yeah?" Jen said.

"Well, Lily looks little!"

Dave's smile turned into a frown.

"Come on, Lily," he said.

"Let's get out of here."

"What's going on?" asked Mrs. Gray.

"I thought Dave was your friend."

Jen burst into tears.

"He was," Jen said.

"Then he got Lily."

"Do you wish you had Lily
instead of Bob?" Mrs. Gray asked.

'Do I?' Jen wondered.

Bob was not as pretty as Lily.

Bob did not run fast like Lily.

But Bob was her Bob.

And Jen loved Bob the Horse.

Bob was an answer to her prayer.

"I'm sorry," Jen told Bob.

"I'm sorry," Jen told God.

"Now I need to tell Dave
I'm sorry, too," she said.

Jen ran to Dave's house.

"I'm sorry I said Lily was little,"
Jen said.

"She really is little," Dave said.

"She is perfect for you!" Jen said.

"And Bob is perfect for me!
God knows how to make
things just right!"

"Do you want to ride Lily?"

Dave asked.

"Yes!" Jen said. "Thanks."

Jen rode pretty Lily fast.

"We can't both ride Lily,"

Dave said. "She's too little."

Jen and Dave still rode

on Bob's big back.

He still was not fast.

But he was Bob the Horse.

And that was just great with Jen.